STEP BY STEP

A linked series of Board Books, Concept Books and Story Books for the pre-school child

Text copyright © 1988 by Diane Wilmer
Illustrations copyright © 1988 by Nicola Smee
First published 1988 by William Collins Sons & Company Ltd.
in association with The Albion Press Ltd.

Aladdin Books
Macmillan Publishing Company
866 Third Avenue, New York, NY 10022

First Aladdin Books edition 1988

Printed in Hong Kong

10   9   8   7   6   5   4   3   2   1

Library of Congress Cataloging-in-Publication Data

Wilmer, Diane.
  Noises.

  (Step by step)
  Summary: All kinds of sounds in and around a busy
household defeat the family's attempts to keep the
baby asleep.
  [1. Noise—Fiction. 2. Sound—Fiction 3. Babies
—Fiction] I. Smee, Nicola, ill. II. Title.
III. Series: Step by step (New York, N.Y.)
PZ7.W685No 1988   [E]   88–16658
ISBN 0–689–71245–6

STEP BY STEP

Noises

Diane Wilmer
illustrated by Nicola Smee

Aladdin Books
MACMILLAN PUBLISHING COMPANY
NEW YORK

Tom's fast asleep.

"Thank goodness," says Mom.

"Let's have a cup of coffee,"
says Dad.

"Mee-ow! Mee-ow!"

"Ssshhh! Jenny!
Baby's asleep."

Chatter. Chatter. Chatter.
That's my sister and her friends
at the door.

"Ssshhh! Claire!
Baby's asleep."

EEEeeeEEEeee!

goes the police car down the street.

"Ssshhh!
Baby's asleep."

CRASH!
BANG!
goes my ball against the fence.

"Ma-ma. Ma-ma."

"Oh, no! Baby's awake."

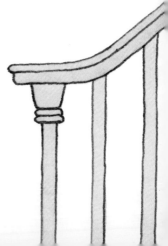

"Peek-a-boo, Tom.
Let's play."